Sherlock Dom

Don't miss the other books in the Definitely Dominguita series!

Definitely DOMINGUITA

Sherlock Dom

By
Terry Catasús Jennings

Illustrated by
Fátima Anaya

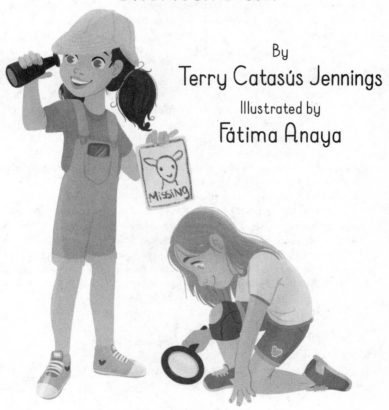

ALADDIN

New York   London   Toronto   Sydney   New Delhi

ALADDIN

An imprint of Simon & Schuster Children's Publishing Division
1230 Avenue of the Americas, New York, New York 10020
First Aladdin hardcover edition November 2021
Text copyright © 2021 by Terry Catasús Jennings
Illustrations copyright © 2021 by Fátima Anaya
Also available in an Aladdin paperback edition.
All rights reserved, including the right of reproduction in whole or in part in any form.
ALADDIN and related logo are registered trademarks of Simon & Schuster, Inc.
For information about special discounts for bulk purchases, please contact
Simon & Schuster Special Sales at 1-866-506-1949 or business@simonandschuster.com.
The Simon & Schuster Speakers Bureau can bring authors to your live event. For more
information or to book an event contact the Simon & Schuster Speakers Bureau
at 1-866-248-3049 or visit our website at www.simonspeakers.com.
Book designed by Heather Palisi
The illustrations for this book were rendered digitally.
The text of this book was set in Candida.
Manufactured in the United States of America 1021 FFG
2 4 6 8 10 9 7 5 3 1
Library of Congress Control Number 2021935654
ISBN 9781534465091 (hc)
ISBN 9781534465084 (pbk)
ISBN 9781534465107 (ebook)

To Cheryl Freeman and Chrissie Devinney
and all who bring children to books
—T. C. J.

To my nephew, Memito
—F. A.

Contents

1
What the Note Said

Dominguita Melendez was up and out the door early on Thursday morning. She was on her way to Yuca, Yuca, the best Cuban restaurant in Mundytown. It was also the only Cuban restaurant in Mundytown. Dom had a deal with the owner, el Señor Prieto: Dom swept the store's sidewalk; el Señor Prieto provided lunch for her crew during their adventures.

Today she hoped el Señor Prieto would give her a lunch-to-go even though the crew wasn't going on an adventure. Just Dom and Steph were going on a weekend trip to Steph's grandmother's house—on the Rappa River.

"It might be the last good food I get till we get back," she told el Señor Prieto.

"You think? Pancho tells me that Steph's grandmother makes great chocolate chip cookies." Pancho was the third member of Dom's crew. He was also el Señor Prieto's nephew.

"Steph called it a cabin . . . out in the country . . . on a river. . . . She said it's next to a marsh." Dom raised her eyebrows. "What if it doesn't even have a kitchen? And you know what? There are no Pizza Palaces out in the country."

"No!"

Dom nodded with force to make sure el Señor Prieto got her point. "By a river? Near a marsh? Nah. No Pizza Palaces."

El Señor Prieto shrugged. He picked out a plate of figure-eight pastries shining with syrup—buñuelos—Dom's and Pancho's favorite food. As if by magic, Pancho stepped out of the restaurant's kitchen.

2

"I wish I could go with you." Pancho reached for one of his uncle's delicious pastries along with a napkin. He was invited, like Dom, to Gran's river house for the long weekend, but his family was going to see his own grandmother.

Dom wanted to make Pancho feel better. She stopped chomping on her buñuelo. "It's not like we'll have any adventures," she said, wiping sticky syrup from her chin. "I couldn't even find the place on the map. *Tapperville!* I'm sure *nothing* will happen there. And we'll be back in no time."

"Just in case." Pancho handed her a piece of paper with his mother's number. "Call me if something happens. I want to be in on the planning. And figuring things out. I want to be part of it all even if I'm not there."

"I'll call you if we get into trouble," she told Pancho. "But really, we won't have any adventures. This place is a million miles from anywhere. Steph and I are taking Sherlock Holmes books. That's about the only excitement we'll have."

Pancho headed home—his shoulders slumped, his head down.

Dom didn't know what to do for him; he looked so sad.

She also didn't know what she would do without him. Before their knightly adventure, Dom hadn't needed friends. She'd found plenty of friends and adventures in her books. But then Pancho had become her squire and Steph, her master of the cookies. She loved her new friends and the adventures she had with them.

Really loved them.

But there was no time to feel sad. She had to get to work. She grabbed the broom and swept the sidewalk. Once she was done, she picked up the bag of food and thanked el Señor Prieto. The smell of ham croquettes and malanga fritters followed her home.

🔍 🔍 🔍

As Dom walked home, she got a call from Abuela. Which was unusual. First because it was early. And second because Abuela now forgot a lot of things. Dom was normally the one to make the calls. But

Abuela sounded sharp today. "It's very important that you behave well," she said. "The family's honor is on your shoulders. And if you don't behave well, that girl, that girl . . ."

"Steph."

"Yeah. Steph. And her grandmother. They'll think Cuban kids don't know how to behave. You're representing Cuban kids everywhere, you know."

The family's honor? Cuban kids everywhere? It was true that Dom had never been away from her family. But really? She was only spending a long weekend! Dom bet her mami had put Abuela up to it.

She was already worried about the food, and now she had to worry about the family's honor and the honor of every Cuban kid in the universe! She had been excited to go, but it was getting complicated.

She was happy that her brother, Rafi, knew exactly what to say when she got home.

"Don't forget," he said. "If you find adventures, take pictures. And take notes. So I can write a book for Abuela . . . *if* you find an adventure."

Steph and her grandmother, Gran, picked Dom up at exactly eight thirty. Which meant Dom's head was still full of warnings when she got in the car. Even though Dom suspected a Mami-Abuela conspiracy, her mami had added to what Abuela said. The warnings ricocheted so fast, she felt her head would explode. And Steph didn't help. She fell asleep two blocks after Dom got in the car.

"Don't you want to take a little snooze?" Gran asked. Dom could see her smile in the rearview mirror. It was clear Gran didn't want to chitchat. Dom took out her phone and added Pancho's number into her contacts.

Mami had given her the phone when Abuela had to move to Miami to live with her sister, because Abuela was forgetting lots and lots of things. Without Abuela, Dom would be home alone after school. At first Dom was supposed to use the phone only to let Mami know she was safe or if she was abducted by aliens. But Dom missed Abuela.

She used the phone to stay in touch. And to solve problems in their adventures. And to take pictures that her brother, Rafi, used to illustrate books he wrote for Abuela. The books were about Dom's adventures—to help Abuela feel like she was still close to Dom and Rafi.

Dom put her phone away. And tried to look out the window. But worry began to snake into her brain. She was good at that. Worrying.

She worried about the cabin. She loved wildlife—during the day. But if a daddy longlegs strolled across her forehead and took a jump on her lips while she was asleep, she might just go through the roof. If a mouse ran across her belly, she would have to burst through the door. That would not be good for the family's honor.

And what if the cabin had no indoor bathrooms? She wasn't looking forward to battling bats and sidestepping snakes to take care of business. She might have to hold it all night to protect the honor of all the Cuban kids who ever existed.

She wished she'd asked Steph a lot more questions

before she'd decided to come. But with Steph asleep, Dom would have to wait until she got to Gran's cabin to know what was what.

The best thing she could do was read.

Dom dove into her favorite Sherlock Holmes story. She didn't come up for air until she felt the car slow down into back roads. They drove through pastures broken by groves of trees. Farm houses, barns, even a few creaky windmills. Cows and sheep and goats. Not at all like the building-crammed streets of Mundytown, where she lived.

After the welcome sign for Tapperville, Gran really slowed down. Dom was happily surprised to see a Pizza Palace as they drove down the main road! Soon Gran turned. Her tires crunched on a long gravel driveway to a beautiful white house. It was a little like Gran's house in Mundytown. Plants dressed in leaves of different greens, yellows, and purples wrapped around a porch that wrapped around the house—a colorful outdoor room with bright yellow rocking chairs. The steps leading to the porch were dark green and shiny.

Is this the house? she mouthed to Steph, who woke when the car slowed down.

Steph nodded.

PHEW!!!!

Gran helped the girls unload the bags and coolers onto the driveway and handed Steph the key.

"I'll be right back," she said.

"We know what to do," Steph said. Then she turned to Dom. "She's going to town to pick up the mail. We can take a minute to look around the yard, but if we take things in, it makes her really happy."

They walked between peach trees and apple trees. Steph showed her Gran's pie patch—raspberry and blueberry bushes bordered with new rhubarb plants.

"Gran and my grandfather used to live here while my grandfather was alive. When he died, my parents talked Gran into moving to Mundytown. But she still spends a lot of time here in the summer."

As Steph showed her around, Dom noted everything in her head. Including a not-so-big gray building that Steph called the barn. Behind it, the marsh seemed to go on forever. And she especially noticed what wasn't there—an outhouse.

"We spend a lot of time in the garden when we're here," Steph explained as they stepped onto the porch. "Did you bring Sherlock Holmes like you said you would?"

Dom nodded. "I read all the way here."

"Gran has a copy. We can come out here and read till she gets back."

"No time for reading," Dom said.

She had seen a note tacked to the door:

ESTHER STOLEN

NEED HELP

2
What Marabella Called Them

"Esther stolen!" Dom's brain spun those two little words like a blender. "That's a job for Sherlock Dom and Steph Watson!" The names came easily, as if she'd been thinking about them for weeks.

Almost three hours of reading Sherlock Holmes had left her itching for a mystery to solve. The huge magnifying glass el Señor Fuentes, the owner of Fuentes Salvage, had given her after their musketeer adventure was carefully stashed in her shoulder bag.

"You know what that means, don't you?" she told Steph, even though she didn't know who Esther was.

"What it means is that Birdie Ballou, Gran's neighbor, lost her nanny goat . . . again," Steph wasn't excited at all. "Esther runs away all the time. Someone always finds her a couple of hours later."

"But still." Dom didn't want to give up. "We could be the ones to find it. To solve the mystery."

"There are no mysteries around this place. Or excitement." Steph started putting the food in the fridge.

"Come on . . . a stolen goat . . ." How could Dom get Steph to understand she wanted a mystery? An adventure?

Steph would not change her mind. They finished stashing the food and put away their clothes in Steph's room. Dom added el Señor Prieto's food to her shoulder bag. Then they toured the house as Steph opened windows and turned on the attic fan.

PHEW, again!!!! So much better than anything Dom had imagined!

The house was airy, even though it was a little

musty from being closed up. Big rooms with huge windows. Bright cushions and pillows. Paintings in light, smudgy colors. Like Gran's house in Mundytown, except that Gran had brought the outdoors in.

And—Dom kept count—it had a grand total of two tubs, three sinks, and three flushing toilets. Plus night-lights. It was a good thing she hadn't told Steph about her cabin fears.

It was past lunchtime, and the ham croquettes and malanga fritters in Dom's shoulder bag were doing a little dance. Now that Dom had seen Gran's kitchen, there was no reason to be afraid she would be going hungry for three days. She brought the treats out of her bag.

"Look what I have. . . ."

Over their adventures, Steph had tried Cuban food and learned to like it. She took Dom's bag and pulled out her share. They sat on the porch.

"Mmmm," Steph said. "Good move to get these. Much better than PB&J."

Dom could only nod; her mouth was so full.

They hadn't been rocking and chomping for very long when an excited woman opened the side gate and rushed toward them, gasping for breath. Her cheeks were full and red. Curly white hair sprang out of a purple bandana around her head. She carried a bag full of carrots. A tall, thin girl slouched along behind her.

"Here's the woman who wrote the note," Dom told Steph. She didn't ask.

"How'd you know?"

"Simple, my dear Watson." Although most people thought Sherlock Holmes said "elementary, my dear Watson," Dom knew that phrase was not in any of his stories. "She's excited because she still hasn't found her goat, has dirty boots from looking in the marsh, and she has a bag of carrots to lure the goat if she finds her. It would have to be her."

"Hello, Mrs. Ballou," Steph said. "This is my friend Dominguita Melendez."

"Hello, hello, hello. Yes, yes, yes. The more, the merrier. Where is Jean? We need all hands on deck. Esther is gone. Lost. Stolen. Who knows? She's never

been gone this long before. And I heard someone's cat has gone missing in town. What if it's an animal-napper? A serial animal-napper? It's a disaster. A pure disaster!" The woman wiped her forehead and kept going to dry her hand on her bandana. She pointed to the girl. "Marabella, here, helps me out. Esther was there when Marabella milked her yesterday afternoon, gone this morning when she came back!"

Marabella rolled her eyes. Dom's guess was that

Marabella was tired of looking for the goat with the old woman.

"Where was Esther when she went missing?" Dom asked. "Can we go there right now?" That was a Sherlock Holmes trick. Look at the scene of the crime right away.

"The pasture, of course. Where else? Oh dear, oh dear, *oh dear*! I don't know where she could be. Don'tknowatall." The last words melted into one.

"We need to search your pasture—"

"No need to search the property, or the one next door, or the field—" The woman wrung her hands. "We've looked at them all, backward and forward. Backward and forward. Back—"

"Yes, ma'am," Steph interrupted. "We get it. Don't need to look."

"But we do," Dom said to Steph. Then she asked the neighbor, "Did you use good detective practices? What clues did you find? What can you tell us?"

"The goat was in the pasture last night, and she wasn't in the pasture this morning. That's what I can say. That's what I can say."

"We looked," Marabella snarled. "The goat's gone. We looked everywhere. The goat's gone from everywhere."

"I'm just saying, if you really want to find your goat . . ." Dom's voice trailed off as if she had a secret she wanted to share.

"Do all you girls from the city think you know it all?" Marabella muttered, and turned away. "How snooty can you get!"

That froze Dom in her tracks. Snooty? Sherlock Holmes's methods worked every time. She narrowed her eyes and shot the girl a look. "I know—"

Steph put a hand on Dom's shoulder to stop her friend. Then she turned to her grandmother's neighbor. "Mrs. Ballou, have you formed search parties? We can join the search parties as soon as Gran gets back."

"Search parties? It would take about three minutes to search Tapperville!" The tall girl flipped back her hair, dismissing Steph.

"Whatever." Steph ignored Marabella. "We'll come to your house as soon as Gran gets back."

But Dom couldn't help herself. She pulled out the magnifying glass from her shoulder bag. "If you want to find something, do what Sherlock Holmes would do."

Marabella snorted. "Such a mighty detective. You gonna use a magnifying glass to find a goat?"

Dom looked at Mrs. Ballou for help, but the neighbor only had thoughts for her goat. "We must continue searching. Tell your grandmother to come over as soon as she gets home."

"You can count on us," Steph said. "Dom and I have actually solved mysteries before."

Marabella sneered.

Which was just enough to make Dom turn her nose up in the air. If Marabella wanted snooty, she'd give her snooty. "Sherlock Dom and Steph Watson will find your goat!" she said to Mrs. Ballou. Then she looked at Steph. "Watson! Let's get ready!"

She and Steph left Marabella and Mrs. Ballou on the porch. They didn't look back.

⚲ ⚲ ⚲

Dom wished she had a true Sherlock Holmes outfit. Some kind of hat. Or a raincoat. But for now they needed to get going. She took out her notebook and pencils from her suitcase. And she also picked up the right half of a pair of binoculars she'd used as a spyglass in their pirate adventures—she'd brought it just in case. Now she was glad she had.

"We need to study the scene," she told Steph as

she arranged the things in her shoulder bag. "We need to do it right now."

"But Mrs. Ballou said they'd already searched the pasture and all the fields."

Oh, man. Dom wished Steph hadn't waited to read Sherlock Holmes until she got to the cabin. "Not how *we'll* search and analyze it. I'm sure they didn't use Sherlock Holmes's ways!"

"Okay," Steph said. "I'll leave Gran a note. I'll tell her about the lost goat and that we want to analyze the scene like Sherlock Holmes."

"Noooo. If she calls, Mrs. Ballou will tell your gran they've already searched the scene. She might make Gran call us back. We won't be able to do a proper inspection."

Steph nodded. "Forget Sherlock. I'll tell her you want to see the barn." She tore a piece of paper from the notebook. "You want to see the whole farm. I'll tell her we won't be long."

"But we might be long," Dom said.

"I'll *tell* her we won't be long!!!"

"Oh . . ."

"I'll ask her to wait until we're back before she goes next door."

Dom sighed and stepped out onto the porch. She loved Sherlock Holmes, and she couldn't wait for Steph to finish so they could examine the scene of the crime.

But the minute her bottom hit the yellow rocking chair, Abuela's voice began to fill her head.

Abuela did not want her to do anything Gran wouldn't like. Would Gran approve of them going to the scene of the crime without being invited? But if they wanted to find the goat, they had to go. What was more important—finding the goat or being invited first?

"We have half an hour," Steph said when she met Dom again on the porch. "That's what I put in the note."

That would have to be enough time.

"We'd better run."

What They Found in the Barns

The first stop was Gran's barn. It was the best way to get to the bigger, reddish barn on Birdie Ballou's property without being seen. Gran's barn was more like a big storage shed. Inside, rakes, shovels, forks, and a wheelbarrow hung neatly on pegs on the wall. Shelves held bins of small garden tools, along with all sorts of pots—some empty, some full of dirt. In one, the skeleton of a dead plant dangled, limp, over the rim.

Hooks lined the other wall. A huge slick raincoat hung from one. Hats hung from others.

Dom stopped. Her eyes twinkled.

Steph picked up the fisherman's rain hat Dom was eyeing—one with a skirt to cover the ears and the neck. "Try it," she urged her detective friend.

Dom hesitated.

"You wore a bucket instead of a knight's helmet for your knightly adventure!"

Dom placed the fisherman's hat on her head, taking care it didn't squish her pigtails. She saw herself in the window. Steph was right. It wasn't like the illustrations of Sherlock Holmes in Abuela's book, but it was awesome!

Steph picked a straw sun hat and plopped it on her own head. She grabbed the big measuring tape and a magnifying glass Gran used to look at bugs on her plants. She put them both in her shoulder bag—the one from their musketeer adventure. The detective team was ready. Time to get to work!

From Gran's barn, a path led to the back of Mrs. Ballou's barn.

The barn wanted to be red, but it really wasn't. It looked like someone had forgotten to add enough color when the paint was mixed. And its roof had wings—like a shore bird about to take off. Dom and Steph hurried over, hugged its side, and crept around to the back.

And they were in luck.

The lock to the back door hung open on the latch.

"We must go in," Dom said, trying to quiet down the *no, no, no!* Abuela's voice was whispering in her head.

"We must!" Steph echoed.

They stepped into the main part of the barn—a wide dirt floor. Empty except for a small platform with a wooden sort of tower on one side.

"That's where Esther climbs up to get milked," Steph explained. "You put her head in that tower thing so she can't get away."

One side of the barn was a goat pen. Dom opened the door and stepped into it. She squatted to check out the floor with her magnifying glass. "I bet Sherlock Holmes never waded through goat poop to do an investigation," she said.

Steph giggled. "Goat berries! Birdie Ballou calls them goat berries. And there's two goats. Esther's the nanny. Albert's the billy. She keeps him because Esther needs to have babies every eighteen months so she can give milk all the time. I bet he's outside."

"How do you know so much about goats?"

"Last summer. I didn't have anything else to do. So she let me milk Esther." Steph scrunched her nose. "I was here two weeks."

Dom was impressed. "You know how to milk a goat?"

Steph shrugged. "Yeah. I bet you when we find Esther, she'll let you milk her."

"What about Marabella?" A thought was creeping into Dom's head.

But Steph coughed and changed the subject. "Let's go up to the loft. I went up there last summer. It's sooo cool."

The idea of going up to the loft made Dom forget her suspicion. "You're right! We might be able to see more from up there. Sherlock Holmes would totally go up there."

Steph scrambled up the ladder. Dom was right behind her.

In the loft, Dom took the left side and Steph took the right. They scanned every inch of floor and wall. Lots of hay but no clues. Not on the floor and the walls. Not on the chute for dropping hay into the feeding trough below. Not even through the magnifying glass.

The girls approached the window. Below them, the marsh made a horseshoe. The wide river took a turn—a shimmering green elbow with diamond flashes from moving water.

"You think a goat could drown in that marsh?" Dom asked.

"Goats don't like water," Steph said with conviction. "She'd never get near it by herself, if that's what you're asking."

"Ponies in *The Hound of the Baskervilles* were sucked up by the mire."

"Is that the story you were reading on the way here?"

"Mm-hmm. Spoo-oo-ooky!"

Steph snickered. "This is a marsh," she said. "Little water paths in between rushes and cattails. It's mushy and oozy, but you can walk on them in low tide. A little ways. Before getting stuck."

"Exactly. Mushy and oozy. Just like the mire in

The Hound of the Baskervilles. I bet you it could suck up a goat."

Steph shrugged.

"And what about those dark smudges on the other side?"

"Lost Town," Steph said. "Gran doesn't let me go there. Marabella says it's haunted."

"Marabella?"

Steph coughed again and looked embarrassed. "I think—"

Dom swept away from the window. The strings on her hat danced. "I'll tell you what *I* think, my dear Watson," she exclaimed. "What *I* think is that last year, when you were here, Marabella was friendly at first. Then Birdie Ballou let you milk the goat because she likes your grandmother. Right so far?"

Steph nodded. There was no mystery there.

But now Dom was ready to share her Sherlock Holmes deduction. "And I bet that made Marabella lose her job."

Steph's mouth dropped. "How . . . ? Why . . . ?"

"And maybe Marabella was counting on the money for something special and she's really mad at you. That's why she called you a snooty city girl!"

"She was saving money for a new hockey-style catcher's helmet. It's much cooler than what the team gives her. She told me that. But how—"

"My dear friend." Dom waved her magnifying glass. "Marabella is just plain unhappy with you. And me. But she was mad at you first."

Steph agreed.

"Then you tell me you milked the goat last summer. And you changed the subject and talked about something else when I was about to ask you what Marabella thought about that. It's clear you felt bad about what happened."

Steph nodded more slowly.

"Then you told me Marabella said Lost Town was a haunted place. So it's plain and simple. You were friends at first. She told you about Tapperville and Lost Town. Then she got mad at you. The only way that would happen is if Birdie Ballou didn't pay her while you were milking the goat and she wanted the money for something special. Did I hit it on the nose, Watson? Like Sherlock Holmes?"

"Just like Sherlock Holmes! The first day, Gran left me with Mrs. Ballou while she went into town. Marabella was there, milking. I spent the rest of the day with her. But then Birdie Ballou showed me how to milk Esther and told Marabella she didn't need to come while I was here. She got M-A-D, MAD. She was ready to buy the helmet in two weeks, but then she had to wait a month. She missed the beginning of the summer season in her new helmet. Gran tried to give her the money, but Marabella's mother said they didn't 'need charity.' She said Marabella could use the team helmet."

"Ooof. Worse than I thought," Dom said. "And *that*, my dear friend, is what makes Marabella suspect number one."

"I don't think so," Steph said. "If Esther's not around, she won't make any money."

"Maybe she'll make money now selling Esther. We know the goat went with someone she knows. *And* she's suspect number one because she's mad at Birdie

Ballou. She's doing it out of spite. And she *could* do it." Dom raised her nose in the air. "Sherlock Holmes would say she had opportunity and motive. Sherlock Dom says it would be easy for her to take Esther."

"Esther's friendly. She'll go with anyone."

"I'm keeping my eye on our girl Marabella, Watson," Dom warned. She pulled out the notebook and divided an open page into three columns. She labeled the first column WHAT WE KNOW. The second she labeled WHAT WE WANT TO KNOW. The last one was for WHAT WE NEED TO FIND OUT. That was the way Dom and her crew solved problems. Writing things down and talking about them. On the column labeled WHAT WE NEED TO FIND OUT, she wrote *Marabella suspect?* "We'll watch her until we rule her out."

"I'm glad you know now." Steph reached for the notebook. "Let me borrow that. I want to be like the real Watson. I'll take notes for us and for Rafi to write our book." She added *Find out if goats go with just anyone* under Dom's note. Then she lay on the floor. "I'll sketch the barn from up here, so we can remember everything."

As Steph sketched, Dom imagined a graph-paper grid over the floor below them. She scanned each square. On the wing opposite the pen, Mrs. Ballou kept supplies on shelves and hanging on hooks. Bottles and bags and jars. Stools and buckets. Milk jugs. Halters and . . . leashes?

Leashes! She took out the spyglass. The things on the walls were made from chains. They ended in leather handles—Dom could see that much. They were bound to be leashes.

"There!" She pointed to the wall below. "I think there's a leash missing from a hook. I'm almost sure of it. . . . I think I see the outline on the wall. It's made from chains."

Steph sprang up from where she was drawing and pointed to the floor below. "Now it makes sense! I didn't know what that scrape in the dirt was. But it could be . . . It could . . ."

"It could be a drag mark from the chain leash!" Dom finished.

"And it keeps going around the stanchion. Where Esther climbs to get milked. See? It ends by

the door to the goat pen." Steph grinned. "Lucky we came up here. We wouldn't have seen it from below. Lots of it's already been erased."

Dom took pictures to add to Steph's sketch.

Below, everything became clear. Dom was right. There were four hooks holding three chain leashes. An oval dust mark showed where the fourth leash would have been.

"And it must have fallen." Dom pointed to a scuffed-up area below the hook and then put her hand up for a high five.

"Wait, wait." Steph pointed to a forked branch lying next to the goat pen door. "Look at that. What if . . . ? What if someone took that branch to lift the chain off the hook? Because they were short. And when they tried to take it down, the leash fell?"

Dom and Steph looked at each other, mouths open, eyes wide. "We have to call Pancho," they said at the same time. There was no way they could leave Pancho out of this.

Dom found Pancho's contact and pressed FaceTime.

"It's a goat. A stolen goat," she said into the screen.

"A goat?" The voice on the other side of the line sounded muffled. All Dom could see was a mass of black hair. The reception was bad—Pancho was probably still on the way to his grandmother's. "Who stole a goat?"

"That's what we need to find out. Who stole a goat?" Dom said.

"Gran's neighbor's goat," Steph added.

"Gran's neighbor's a goat?"

"No, the neighbor's goat got stolen!"

"Who's Gran?"

"What do you mean who's Gran? Steph's grandmother. And it could get swallowed in the mire like the ponies in *The Hound of the Baskervilles*," Dom added.

"Not a mire," Steph said. "A marsh."

"Your grandmother's gonna be swallowed by the marsh?"

"The mire! And Esther, Esther the goat. Not Steph's grandmother. She doesn't go on the marsh . . . or on the mire."

"So how will she get swallowed by the mire or the marsh if she doesn't go on it?"

"Hand me that phone, Pete," a clear Pancho voice said.

"Wait!" Now Dom saw the whole face. It wasn't Pancho. And the boy was laughing.

He passed the phone to the back seat. "Here you go, bro. I think it's Sherlock Holmes, but it's a girl, and she's wearing a goofy hat."

"Sherlock Dom, and it's not a goofy hat!" Dom barked into the phone.

"Sherlock Holmes wore a deerstalker hat," Pancho's brother's voice said in the distance.

"An illustrator decided that," Pancho corrected his brother. "None of the books ever said what kind of hat Holmes wore."

"Whatever, bro. Just don't talk loud, okay?"

Dom couldn't wait to tell Pancho. "The minute we got here we found an adventure!"

"A stolen goat," Steph chimed in.

"And Steph's gran lives on a marsh just like the mire of *The Hound of the Baskervilles*."

"Oh, man! *The Hound of the Baskervilles!*"

Dom smiled. They should have brought Pancho in the minute they heard Esther was missing.

They explained everything. And texted him pictures. Dom put Pancho back in her front pocket and climbed the ladder to the loft. She showed him the marsh. And the black things on the other side of the marsh.

"Yeah," Pancho said. "I looked it up. Marsh and mire. They're the same thing. Oozy things that can swallow you. And maybe those dark things are like the prehistoric huts, like in *The Hound.*"

"It's called Lost Town. But Marabella, our number one suspect, thinks it's a haunted place. It's right on the edge between the marsh and a big meadow, you know, like the moor." Dom then panned across the whole barn. She and Steph pointed out what they'd found.

"Awesome . . . Okay, got it. . . . And you didn't think this was going to be exciting." Pancho babbled as they explained everything.

Back downstairs, they showed him the hooks and the scrape and the shelves.

"Stop," Pancho said. "Zoom. Zoom in on that shelf with the buckets."

Dom zoomed, but she didn't have to. She and Steph now saw exactly what Pancho had spied.

"One of the buckets is missing," Steph said.

"Whoever took Esther is planning on milking her."

"Whoever took Esther is planning on keeping her for a long time."

"But not forever," Dom said. "If you were planning on keeping her forever, you'd have to have a place like this." She spread her arms to take in the whole barn. "And you'd need lots of buckets and bottles and jars. . . ."

"Not if you sell her for meat . . . ," Pancho said.

"MEAT!" Both Steph and Dom cringed when they yelled the word.

When Dom said Marabella might want to sell Esther, she'd thought it was for a pet . . . or for milk. . . . What if someone had already taken Esther and made her into goatburger?

"Wait. If the thief wanted to . . . you know . . ." Steph couldn't bring herself to say it. "Anyway, taking the milk bucket means the thief's planning to keep her alive. At least for a little while. So we have to find her quickly. Just in case!"

"That's why we must use Sherlock Holmes's methods!"

"Let's keep going." Steph led the way.

They kept Pancho on FaceTime while they quickly used the magnifying glasses to examine the small door from the goat pen to the pasture.

They examined the ground, careful to make sure they couldn't be seen from Mrs. Ballou's house.

"No sign of struggle," Dom said.

The others agreed.

"Man," Pancho said. "That's why it's so important to get to the scene of the crime right away."

Dom agreed. "All clues erased, I'm sure, by Birdie's boots and Marabella's flip-flops."

"You noticed their shoes?" Steph asked.

Dom nodded, proud of being a good detective.

They walked from one side of the barn's main door to the other, scanning the pasture in front of them, looking for Albert and for clues.

Two climbing towers and four garbage cans—some upside down, others lying on the ground—dotted the pasture. At one time or another, the cans had been butted by goat horns. The goats could drink water from buckets under pump faucets. And the goats could get away from the sun in a little lean-to close to the right of the pasture.

That's where Albert was. Munching and resting.

"So that's what Esther looks like?" Pancho said. The billy goat had golden hair, flattish curly horns, and a white beard.

"Pancho and Dom," Steph said. "Meet Albert. He's got really long hair. See his beard?"

"Look . . ." Dom wanted to *ooh* and *aah* over Albert, but they had things to do. "We'd best get going to the marsh. We don't have much time left."

"I don't think you'll find any clues in the pasture

anyhow," Pancho said from the phone. "I bet Albert already erased them."

They crept to the pasture gate on hands and knees, with Pancho in Dom's pocket. Dom popped up to check and see if anyone had seen them.

She couldn't see Mrs. Ballou's house, so she was sure Mrs. Ballou couldn't see them. They examined the gate and saw no signs of struggle in the dirt around it.

Then they cut across a corner of Mrs. Ballou's yard to the closest edge of the marsh. The backyard grass was freshly cut. Even if they were able to look there without being seen, they had little hope of finding hoofprints, or traces of the chain leash.

"Our best chance is in the marsh," Dom told the crew.

They crouch-walked on a strip of black dirt. On one side of the strip, cattails and water hibiscus hid them from the houses. On the other, water crept toward them. The ground was just a little mushy, but not enough to make their shoes sink in. Not deep. If the goat and her captor had been through there, they should have been able to see prints. But there were none.

Dom took Pancho out of her pocket and held him up between the tops of the cattails. "Tell us what you see."

"You're exactly behind a house. Is it Birdie's house? You're behind the back porch and . . . Get me down! Get me down! Someone's coming out."

Dom jerked her phone and Pancho down. They crouched lower. And as she turned back to the marsh, her heart stopped.

"Goat berries!" she whisper-screamed. "And hoofprints—" The clues were about four feet ahead of them. But they were perfectly clear. "You see them?"

"Hey, you two!" The voice from Mrs. Ballou's back porch was Marabella's.

Caught! Dom and Steph stood up. Marabella was pointing right at them.

They stood still for a couple of seconds. Then, with a wild yell, Dom took a step, a leap, and a spectacular fall. She ended up next to the prints. Luckily, with Pancho still in her hand and Gran's hat still on her head.

"Do you see that?" she said, showing Pancho the evidence.

"Yes. You have it. Perfect!" Pancho said.

Dom got on her hands and knees and raised a hand. The one without the phone.

"Just a little fall," she yelled. "Just stepped in the wrong place. . . . We'll be joining you . . . as soon as I change into clean clothes."

Then she rose slowly. Standing with her back to the house, she positioned her phone. And captured the whole scene. She focused on the hoofprints.

Click. And on the goat berries. *Click.* And on three small circles. *Click.* Stepping back toward Steph, she handed the phone to her friend. Instead of Pancho, the screen showed clear pictures of goat berries, two hoofprints, a trace of chain, and a very clear print with the three telltale circles of a flip-flop. The sole of the flip-flop was cracked. In a zigzag. From the edge almost to the middle of the shoe.

"You did it!" Steph said. "An unmistakable clue!"

"And taking a fall so you can analyze evidence without anyone knowing? Very much like Sherlock Holmes." Pancho's voice joined them.

"Now we know for sure that Esther didn't run away," Steph said.

"She was stolen!" Dom finished.

They shifted the screen back to Pancho. "Inspector Pancho here," he said, pretending to be one of the police detectives who were often part of Sherlock Holmes's adventures. The trio was going places together, even though Pancho was miles away from his friends.

4
What They Know and Don't Know

They didn't need to hide anymore. They ran back to Gran's house at full speed. While Dom cleaned up at the hose, they chattered. All three of them. Pancho was still on the line.

"We'll have to figure it out . . . ," Steph said.

"What we know and what we don't know," Pancho added from the phone.

"And make our plan," Dom finished as she

46

scrubbed her left knee. She was happy to be back solving problems with her whole crew.

"What about Gran?" Steph said. "She wants us now—to look for the goat."

"We'll just have to tell her what we've seen," Dom said. "Ask her to let us wait until we have a plan."

"She'll agree," Steph said. "She has to."

And Gran did agree. "I'll go make a cup of tea to calm Mrs. Ballou. You two meet me at her house as soon as you can. Nice to see you, Pancho." Gran waved at the screen as she left the porch.

Steph and Dom sat on Gran's back porch with the notebook spread before them. Pancho looked on from the phone.

"So, we're sure Esther went with someone she knows, " Dom said, and started to erase what they'd written in the WHAT WE NEED TO FIND OUT column.

"I don't think we're sure," Steph said. "I think we should leave that where it is. We need to find out if that's true."

"I agree," Pancho said.

Dom stopped erasing.

"But we do know whoever took her is small," Steph said.

That surprised Dom. "That's Marabella's print! She's not small."

"Nope. The flip-flop print in the marsh mud was small. Look at the picture. Your hand landed next to the flip-flop print when you fell."

"So?" Dom wanted the flip-flop print to be Marabella's. In her mind, all they'd have to do was ask Birdie Ballou to get Marabella to take off her flip-flops to solve the crime.

Steph stuck to her own idea. "The flip-flop print wasn't much longer than your hand. I think it's a little kid's print. A little kid took the goat."

Dom pulled up the picture while keeping Pancho on the line. "I wish we could have measured it. So it's not Marabella's footprint?"

"I saw what Steph saw," Pancho said. "And you told me that whoever picked up the leash from the hook used a branch to do it. If we believe that, then we have to believe that person was short. A little kid is short. Probably younger than we are."

Dom had to agree. "Okay. I'll give you that. The person who took her was short. Probably a little kid." She scribbled on the WHAT WE KNOW column. She also wrote down that the right flip-flop had a zigzag crack on the bottom.

When she finished, she glanced at Steph. "But I still think Marabella's a suspect."

"No problem there," Pancho agreed. "They can both be true. We just don't have proof about Marabella. . . ."

"*Yet!*" Dom finished. "So I'm leaving Marabella under WHAT WE NEED TO FIND OUT."

"Another thing you need to do is go around town and figure out if there's a place where Esther could be hidden."

"Would it have to be in town?" Dom said. "Could someone have taken her to a farm outside of town?"

"I don't think so," Steph answered. She picked up the phone and panned along, showing Pancho a group of small houses directly in front of them, on the other side of a wide field. As she panned, she pointed with her other hand, so Dom could see. "That's Tapperville. Three blocks long. Four or five blocks wide. On this side of the field, there's Marsh Coast Road." She pointed it out to both Dom and Pancho. "Houses like Gran's go from the marsh to the Marsh Road." She kept showing Pancho on the phone. "See? They all have long driveways. People around here call it the Marsh Strip."

"Good name," Pancho said.

"But what about the farms?" Dom remembered what she saw on the way to Tapperville.

"They're so big. With lots of buildings and land. And cattle and sheep and goats. If someone took Esther out to a farm, we'll never find her. It would take too long."

"But it makes sense to concentrate in town and in this neighborhood."

"In town only," Steph corrected. "Mrs. Ballou has an Esther alert. The minute Esther leaves, she sends a text around the Marsh Strip. Everyone's her friend. They tell her if they've seen Esther."

"Okay. Number one: find out if Esther's in town. Then we need to figure out if goats will go with just anyone, or if they'd get upset by a stranger. That could point the finger at Marabella. Everybody else would be a stranger, right? And we need to find the little flip-flop with the zigzag crack."

"We'll just have to look at the feet of all the little kids we meet."

"And we still need to keep our eye on Marabella." Dom was convinced that even if Marabella wasn't the main culprit, she knew something about the theft. Maybe a lot about it.

As Steph shut the notebook and put it in her shoulder bag, the sounds of loud voices and car doors filled the phone.

"Gotta go," Pancho said. "I'll try to check the internet for how goats behave. Good luck!" As Pancho hung up, Dom's home screen came up—a picture of her reading with Abuela.

"Sherlock Dom and Steph Watson—ready to search Tapperville!" Dom said when they entered Mrs. Ballou's porch. She looked around for Marabella, but their number one suspect was gone.

"Marabella?" Gran asked. "She went home. Mrs. Ballou is calmer now. She knows we're doing all that can be done. Marabella said she'd look in town, and it's a good idea if the two of you do the same. Be back by five o'clock, but remember, don't go to Lost Town."

The girls walked on a path straight through the field of tall grass that separated the Marsh Strip from Tapperville's tiny downtown.

They hadn't been walking very long when they caught a movement on the street straight in front of them.

"Duck!" Dom said.

Both girls hit the dirt, breathless, trying to make themselves smaller than the tall blades of grass around them.

"Marabella and a little boy," Dom said.

Steph panted. "I saw them!"

"We need to check that flip-flop!"

"But if we run, they'll see us."

"If we don't run, we can't check the flip-flop."

They ran.

But they didn't find anyone. Or anything.

Not Marabella. Not the little boy. Not a cracked flip-flop. They had vanished.

They checked up and down streets, where they found . . . nothing. They checked front yards and backyards. They checked mud puddles for prints. They sniffed the air, in case a goat-ish kind of smell might by chance find their nostrils. Nothing.

They even peeked through windows. With Dom's spyglass. Which was not a good idea.

An old man came out of his house. "You spying on me?" he said. "Do I need to call the police?"

"No, no, no!" Steph said. "Just looking for the goat. Mrs. Ballou's goat."

"Honest!" Dom put away the spyglass and put on her most innocent look. She couldn't be caught spying. It would be awful for the honor of Cuban children everywhere.

They stopped at the grocery store and talked to

the produce manager. Someone who stole a goat would have to feed it, right? Maybe Marabella and Cracked Flip-Flop Boy bought some greens to feed Esther. That would be proof enough.

"Anybody come here to get food for a goat?" Dom asked the produce manager.

"Oh yes," the man said. "Mrs. Ballou got a big bag of carrots."

"No one else?" Steph asked. "Like a blond girl about twelve and a little boy?"

"It's not a huge store, but I've only seen my regulars."

They checked the alley behind the grocery store, where there might be food in the trash. Maybe Marabella and Cracked Flip-Flop Boy scavenged the trash cans. But there were no flip-flop prints, with or without cracks. And no goat prints or goat berries, either. And there would have been, if the villains and their prey had walked there—the alley was caked in mud.

A vet's office was next to the grocery store.

"Anyone been asking questions about goats?"

Dom asked the lady behind the counter. She thought that was a good way to start the conversation.

"If you mean other than Mrs. Ballou calling to see if we'd seen Esther, no." The woman who spoke had just come through a door next to the counter. She had on a plaid shirt, rubber boots, jeans, and red glasses that covered just about her whole face. She laughed from the bottom of her belly. "She's already called me three times today."

Dom made the introductions. "Sherlock Dom and Steph Watson. Steph here, her gran lives next to Mrs. Ballou. We're trying to help find Esther. We have some clues, but we need more information."

"Ah, yes. The out-of-towners. Birdie told me you would be helping." She pulled a book off the counter and began leafing through it. "Let's see. My last critter's due in at three fifteen. How 'bout y'all mosey over around four? I'll answer all your questions."

"Thank you, thank you," Dom and Steph said at the same time.

The sun seemed a little brighter when they came out of the vet's office. They would be finding out the answers to some of their questions. So, with a tad more hope, Sherlock Dom and Steph Watson continued their quest.

Behind the Tapperville Rec Center, they found a short metal building with seven compartments—each big enough to hide a goat. *Big enough to hide a goat!*

One was labeled SOFTBALL. One SOCCER. Two were labeled BASEBALL. One just said EQUIPMENT. Two had no name. Most were secured with combination locks.

The girls sneaked into the two without locks. They were empty except for mouse droppings.

"Let's concentrate on the ones that are not labeled," Steph said.

"You mean you wouldn't hide a goat in a place full of baseball equipment?"

Steph smiled. "Duh!"

"But what if the criminal moved the baseball stuff or the soccer stuff and put a goat in there? No one but us would think of looking for Esther in a place people normally use for storing sports equipment, right?"

Steph had to agree with that. No one but them.

"I don't see any windows in these things. Esther will die if she can't breathe."

That stopped Dom.

For a second.

"Maybe there's a window we can't see on the other side—the side right next to the building, or maybe they have a fan on the roof to bring air in and out?"

Steph hadn't seen any windows in the two empty compartments, and no fans for sure. But there was no harm in studying all the doors—labeled and not labeled.

They inspected the ground for hoofprints. Nothing. They examined the doors and their locks through their magnifying glasses. Not a clue. They sniffed for Esther. Not a whiff.

In the first four.

But at the fifth one . . . the one labeled SOFTBALL . . . a hair peeked at them from the latch. A blond hair. Dom unraveled it carefully from the metal catch.

"Marabella's," Dom said. "I'm sure." She put it in one of the Baggies they'd brought to store evidence.

Then she sniffed the door.

"I'm catching a goat-ish smell," Dom whispered. She got on her hands and knees to smell the lower part of the door. "Yes. I definitely smell it."

Steph also got down and took in a great big breath. The girls were so occupied that they didn't hear footsteps next to them.

"I never heard of Sherlock Holmes using his nose to find a goat!"

Both girls jumped. The mocking voice was Marabella's.

Caught!

"Sherlock Holmes used all his senses. We were searching . . ."

"On your hands and knees? Like puppy dogs?"

"We-e-e-l-l-l," Dom said. "Sherlock Dom and Steph Watson have their ways. We're looking for Esther, and we're gonna find her." Dom raised her eyebrows so Marabella would know she was a suspect. "We found a hair. A blond hair. And this place smells like goat. Maybe you put Esther in there."

"You think it's my hair? You think I hid Esther in there?"

"We know it's yours," Dom lied. Sometimes Sherlock Holmes made up things to get the suspects to confess. She stood up and pulled out the Baggie with the blond hair.

"And you didn't think that maybe I play softball and get equipment out of this shed all the time? And

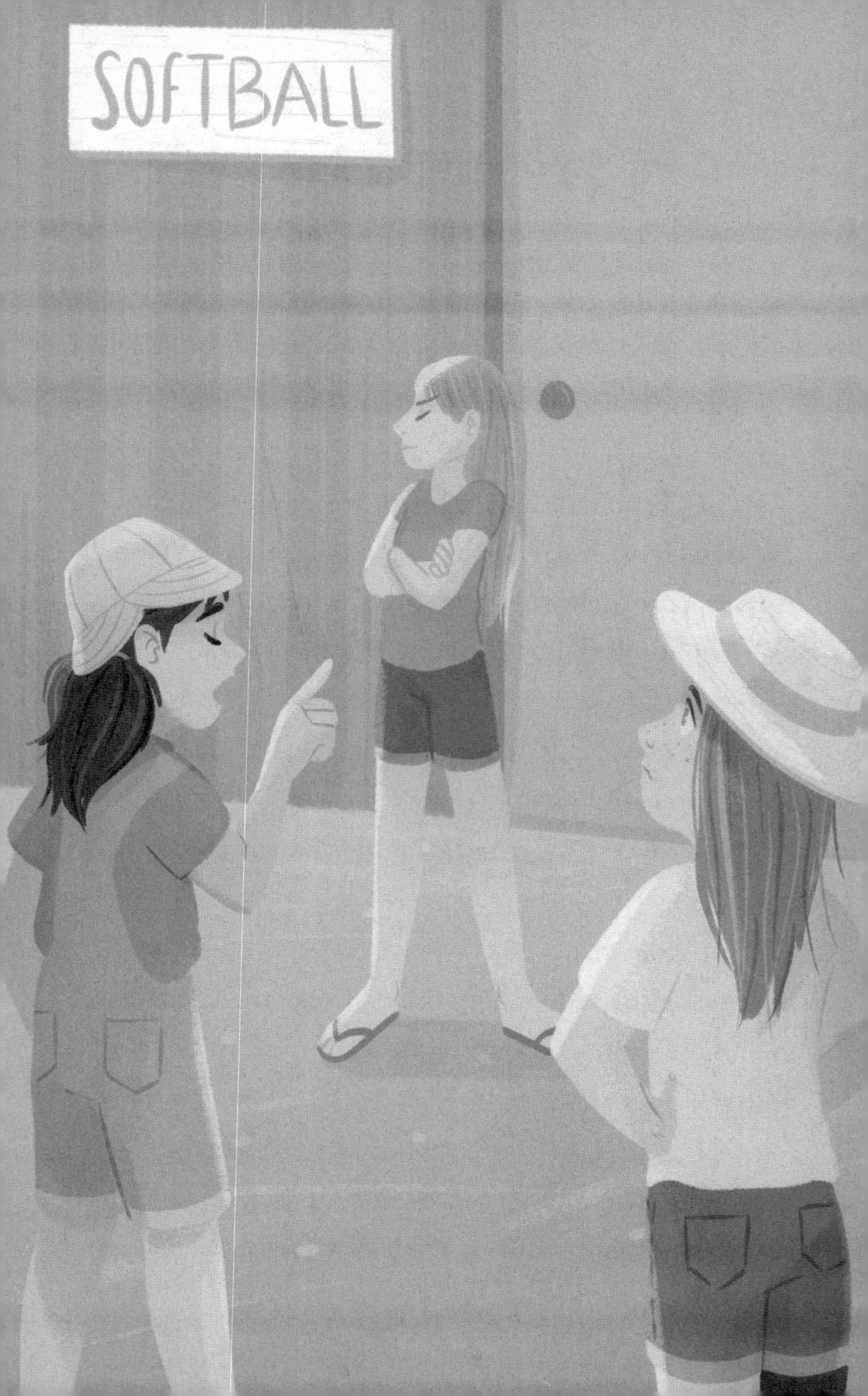
SOFTBALL

you didn't think that sweaty catcher's equipment and cleats smell even worse than goats?" Marabella challenged the two detectives.

Of course Dom hadn't thought of that. But even if that was true, Marabella could still be one of the thieves. Dom huffed. She could tell a whopper for a good cause, but she still hesitated a minute. "We have proof. And it's not just you."

Steph's mouth dropped.

But not Marabella's. "Awwww. The itty-bitty detective has proof! I'm so scared. I'm a suspect. You walked the whole town and you didn't find anything. Where do you think it is, out on the moor? Oh, please, please, Sherlock. Don't take me to jail."

Dom wagged her finger at the blond girl. "You just wait."

"I'm shaking in my flip-flops!" Marabella turned her nose up in the air and left Steph and Dom stunned.

What could they do?

As if Dom had summoned him, Pancho rang on her phone.

"I blabbed, Pancho," Dom said. "Again." During their pirate adventure Dom had been a real blabber, and it got them into trouble!

Steph didn't try to make her feel better.

"So, tell me what happened," Pancho said.

The girls did.

Pancho stared from the phone for a few seconds before he spoke. "You did tell her that she was a suspect, but I think she already knew that."

"She knew," Steph agreed after a second. "She knows we saw her with the little boy. She knows we looked everywhere in town. She knows we were in the marsh. She probably knows we saw the prints."

PHEW!!! Maybe she didn't make a total mess of things.

"Can you stick around?" Dom asked Pancho. "We're heading to see the town vet right now."

"I can," Pancho said. "But first wait. Did you say that Marabella girl talked about the moor?"

Dom and Steph stopped walking and concentrated on the phone.

"Oh," Dom said. "I think she said the moor, but maybe I'm too much into Sherlock Holmes."

"I heard it," Steph confirmed. "I was about to say something when Pancho called. She definitely said *moor*."

Pancho spoke again. "Soooo. Moors are in England. Here we have grasslands, meadows, and pastures." Pancho shook his head so hard that Dom almost felt it through the phone. "We don't have moors. She's read Sherlock Holmes. She's playing a game with us."

Steph thought for a second. "But she took the goat before we got here."

"Yes," Dom said. "But Pancho's right. Maybe she wasn't thinking about *The Hound* before, but she's thinking about it now. And that tells us the goat is on the moor! I bet it's that place on the other side of the marsh. That Lost Town. Maybe she *is* playing a game with us."

"Or maybe she figures if she points the finger at the moor, we won't go there," Steph said. "Backward thinking to throw us off the scent."

"Of course!" Pancho said what both the girls were thinking. "Either way, she's thinking of the moor because she's thinking of *The Hound*."

"And Lost Town doesn't belong to anyone. So no one would check there." Steph was almost jumping out of her skin.

Dom high-fived Steph and the phone. "So we know who did it."

"Kind of," Steph added. "We know Marabella's in on it, and there's probably a little boy along with her."

"And we know where the goat is."

"We're pretty sure we know," Steph and Pancho said at the same time.

"Now all we have to do is find exactly where she is, find out why, and find the little boy."

"That's all we have to do," Steph said.

"Simple, my dear Watson. Simple."

What the Vet Told Them

Dom showed Pancho an old framed map at the vet's office.

"Here is the town." She pointed. "And here is the strip of land that has lots of houses now. It didn't then. Gran's house is about here. And here is the marsh—the horseshoe. And there is Lost Town."

"Lost Town was ruined by a flood about one hundred years ago." Dr. Cabrera's voice answered the question in Dom's mind. "Y'all come on back. I'm free now."

Dom and Steph found seats in a bright teal room. Bookshelves groaning under the weight of a gazillion books lined the walls. A plastic skeleton of a dog filled a shallow counter next to her desk. On the desk was a picture of a goat with a blue ribbon attached to its collar.

They placed Pancho on the vet's desk, propped up on a pile of folders.

"We had an escaped convict in Lost Town, oh, I don't know, about sixty years ago. Before I was born. Way before. My grandfather was the one who found him. He was looking for birds through his telescope. Instead, he found a man hiding."

Dom gasped. "A desperate criminal?"

The vet threw back her head and laughed. Her whole body shook. "Had to be desperate—to hole up in a place like Lost Town." She wiggled her eyebrows. "Most people say it's haunted."

"Do you think it's haunted?" Steph asked.

Dr. Cabrera shrugged. She became serious. "Half-

and-half, I guess. I never minded playing there when I was a kid. It was a great place for hide-and-seek. One night when I was in high school, a bunch of us went there after dark. Oh, the moans and the groans and the whistles. People in town say it's the souls of those who died in the flood, way back when. I don't know what it was, but we didn't last long that night. My dad said it was just the wind blowing through the piles of wood in the ruins. Me?" Her eyebrows jumped again. "I don't go there at night unless I need to rescue some critter. And even then I take a friend."

Dom wanted more answers. "Let's get back to the convict. Did he get swallowed by the mire?"

"You mean like in *The Hound of the Baskervilles*?"

The girls nodded. Pancho gave a thumbs-up.

"No, no. Actually, it ended up being a good story. I still have the clipping from the paper. He was a thief, all right, and he was desperate, all right. But he was desperate because he couldn't see his children. And he had stolen because he'd lost his job. He had no food to feed them. The town came together. They paid back what he'd stolen. And everyone pitched

in to take care of the kids. I think . . . I think one was fourteen and one was ten. Anyway, he became a teacher when he got out of jail."

Dom, Steph, and Pancho were all quiet when Dr. Cabrera stopped talking. But she wasn't finished.

"I'm very proud of my grandfather," she said. "He

was the one who pulled the town together to help the man." She took a deep breath, as if to bring herself back to the present. "So, now, I'm ready to answer all the questions you have. I love goats. And it's not just because I'm a vet." She pointed to the picture in front of her. "That's Esther's mother. I won a blue ribbon in 4H with her when I was ten. Esther and I are related." The vet leaned back on her cushy chair, stretched, and stomped her feet before she crossed them. "So you're Jean Williams's granddaughter." Her eyes moved from Steph to Dom. "And you're her friend from Mundytown. Welcome to tiny Tapperville."

"Don't forget me." Pancho's voice came from the phone. "I'm Pancho Sanchez, also from Mundytown."

"Pleased to make your acquaintance." She nodded to the phone. "And now, how can I help you?"

All three asked the questions they'd written down, and Dr. Cabrera answered. By the time they left, they knew that Esther probably went with someone she knew. Goats aren't all that crazy about strangers.

"She would have planted her feet or pawed the ground. You would have been able to see signs of a scuffle on the ground. She might have even made a ruckus," Dr. Cabrera said. "And no, Esther wouldn't have gone to the marsh unless someone led her there. Goats hate water."

They learned that Esther often wandered off because Mrs. Ballou had a habit of forgetting to latch the gate.

"Albert's much older and content to stay where he is," Dr. Cabrera said. "I was actually trying to make time to look for Esther myself. She should have been home by now."

"Do you think someone took Esther?"

"What I'm more afraid of is that she might find herself in Lost Town at night and get hurt."

"Oh!" Dom agreed with the vet on one thing. Esther was in Lost Town. But she didn't agree that Esther might have wandered there by herself. "We think that someone took Esther." She showed Dr. Cabrera the picture of the prints on her phone after she let Pancho know what she was doing.

"Mmm. Interesting."

"Do you know a girl named Marabella?" Dom asked the vet.

"Ah, Marabella Reed. Yes, I do. She's the star slugger for . . ."

Dom didn't let her finish the sentence. "We think Marabella's in on the crime. We have evidence."

"Evidence, huh?" The vet leaned in toward Dom. "I would be surprised if that were the case. Marabella's a little gruff on the outside, but . . ."

"She was nasty to us," Dom declared.

Dr. Cabrera cocked her head to one side. "Well, our Marabella might have got your goat, like people say, but that doesn't mean she'd steal. And it doesn't make sense. Birdie pays her well for milking Esther." The vet scrunched her forehead. "I'd be careful. Get to know more facts before calling Marabella a thief."

The words gave Dom a shiver. Had she been tracking the wrong suspect all along? NO! Maybe Marabella wasn't a thief, but she knew something about what happened to Esther. She looked at her two friends. An idea was forming in her head. They had to go. "Do we have any more questions?"

Steph shook her head.

"Not me. Thank you, Dr. Cabrera!" Pancho said from the phone.

"Here's my cell number." The vet handed Dom and Steph cards. "I give this to the parents of all my critters. Thanks for helping Birdie. I love that old goat. And Esther too." The vet laughed at her own joke. "I hope you find her. Call me if there's anything I can do. Anything. I'll be happy to help you."

"Thank you. Thank you," Steph said. "We'll let you know if we find anything."

Dom was so excited to be leaving that she forgot Pancho and had to go back to fetch him.

What Happened in Lost Town

It was four thirty and Pancho had to go with his family. Dom and Steph said goodbye and called Gran to ask for half an hour more. "We're hot on the trail," Dom said. What she didn't say was that she had convinced Steph they had to go to Lost Town. She was sure Gran wouldn't agree to that.

They stopped at the top of the horseshoe—where the Marsh Coast Road ended. From there, a path led through tall grass. They could see the ruins of Lost

Town. Dom figured it was about five blocks, even though there were no streets. She took out her spyglass and looked all around. She could see the ruins clearly. Walls and half walls—made of rocks or crumbling bricks—some even with holes that would have been windows. Rotten wood piles. Pieces of metal, which could have been tin roofs. But no goats. As she put the spyglass back in her shoulder bag, she pointed to a home very close to where they stood.

"That's Dr. Cabrera's house. I'm sure." She pointed to the driveway. "I can see a picture of a goat on the mailbox. There's a telescope on the back porch."

Steph scrunched her nose. "Could be."

They headed down the path. Most of the time they walked on matted grass. They looked for hoofprints. Or goat berries. They weren't looking for what they heard.

A howl.

A loud howl.

It sounded again, a terrible call that sent shivers down both girls' spines.

They walked a few more steps and stopped—again—at the sound of two more howls.

"Do you think it's a hound, like in the story? Tied up in Lost Town?"

"I don't know," Dom said, happy that Steph remembered the story. "Something doesn't sound right. Do you know of any hounds in Tapperville?"

Steph shook her head. "I don't know about a hound. But maybe a dog? A wild dog that could bite us."

In the book, the villain had tied up a hound in a cave next to the mire. He didn't feed it. And he covered the hound's muzzle with glow stuff. When the man finally let it loose, the hound was crazy. It attacked the first person it saw. The person he attacked died of fright; the dog was so scary!

"You think Marabella would tie up a dog to scare us?"

Steph shook her head.

"And the sound. That howl didn't sound normal."

"You mean supernatural?"

"No . . . It was something . . . You know how it repeated? It didn't sound real. It was one howl and then the second one. And then the next time, it repeated exactly the same way."

"You mean like a recording?"

"Could be, Watson!"

"Yeah!" Steph nodded, as if she'd made a decision. "We don't have to worry, then."

The good feeling lasted until Steph pointed to a place off the path. There were definitely signs of a struggle. Matted-down grass. Hair. Traces of something dark.

"No!" Dom wasn't sure she wanted to ask the next question. "Esther?"

Her eyes met Steph's. It couldn't be Esther! How could they tell Mrs. Ballou?

Dom joined Steph and squatted to analyze the scene. "Looks like there are footprints here too. Gosh, I'm not sure."

"I think if it were Esther, more grass would be messed up, you know? Esther's big. This is a struggle with a small animal. Maybe it's a fox, hunting. Remember Mrs. Ballou said some cat was missing?"

"Ugh," Dom said. "Maybe that was it."

"I'll take a look," Steph said. "I'll follow this. Maybe I can see more hair or something. Let me take your phone so I can take pics of anything I find. I'll be right back."

While Steph followed the trail, crouching with her magnifying glass, Dom stayed behind. She stood and pulled out her spyglass and searched—all around. Even back toward the Marsh Strip. Maybe she was looking for the fox. But maybe she was also trying to get used to Steph being so much in charge. She looked at her phone. They only had thirty minutes left.

As she was putting her phone away, she heard the howls. Very loud. Very close. She ran toward the sound, hoping to find it.

And plunged.

Chest-deep.

Into a sandy hole.

"HELP! STEPH, HELP!"

The howls repeated. So loud, Dom was sure Steph

couldn't hear her. She tried to wave her arms, but the dirt kept shifting. Was it quicksand? "STEPH!"

She tried to pull herself out, but every time she tried to move, the sand shifted around her. There was no way to push off to pull herself out of the hole. And Steph wasn't answering her.

The howl echoed through the sandy bog again. Where was Steph? Dom couldn't see through the weeds.

She heard heavy tramping. Panting. Brush being moved. The hound . . . ? Something gripped her arm and pulled. Then she was being lifted—up and out. "Dr. Cabrera!"

"I told you Lost Town wasn't haunted . . . when we talked," she said, gasping. "But—but—I didn't tell you it wasn't dangerous!"

They sat on the grass, both of them trying to catch their breath. Dom had never been so scared in her life, but she did notice Dr. Cabrera had used a double negative perfectly.

"Let me look at you." The vet tried to make Dom lie back. But Dom didn't want to.

She stood up. "Steph. Where is Steph?"

"I saw her on my way here. Now try to walk. Anything hurt?"

Dom shook her head. Sand poured from her clothes.

"You'll have a nice bruise there on your leg. But it could have been a lot worse."

Dom heard the sound of grass being trampled and finally saw her friend running toward them. "Steph!"

"What's going on?" Steph's eyes were huge. "Dom! You look awful!"

"Sherlock Dom took a tumble," Dr. Cabrera said. "But I think the worst we have is some torn coveralls and a two-steak bruise. And two someones who I hope won't go off traipsing where they shouldn't ever again."

Dom finally said what she'd been thinking. "Was—was that quicksand?"

"Nah. Just a hole. Probably covered with grass. You're lucky it wasn't deep and that I decided to take a look for Esther when I got home."

"I'm sorry," Steph said. "We shouldn't have gone

into Lost Town, but we saw signs of a scuffle. Maybe a fox. And we were afraid for Esther."

"I know. I know you're trying to find Esther and the only place left was Lost Town," the vet said. "I get it. That's what I thought too. But you shouldn't have come alone."

"Well." Steph reached carefully into her bag. "I found something." When her hands came out, they held an orange tabby kitten. Tiny and scared.

Dr. Cabrera picked up the tiny ball of orange fur. "Awwww."

"Is he . . . ? Is he all right?"

"Hungry, I'm sure. Come on, baby," she said. "We'll take you to my house and feed you. I have some goat milk in my freezer at the office. Perfect for you. We'll get you chasing mice in no time."

"I followed a trail through the grass," Steph said. "And I saw hair. Orange hair. I took pictures, and I kept going. What if it was Esther, right? Then I heard a faint meow."

"Why didn't you yell?" Dom said, although maybe by that time she was already deep in the hole.

"The howling. It was so loud. I wasn't scared. But I knew you couldn't hear me until it ended. That's when I saw Dr. Cabrera running. And I couldn't see you. And I panicked and started running toward her."

As they walked back, Steph and Dr. Cabrera talked about the kitten.

"I think the mama cat was chased away by a fox," Steph said. "Or worse."

Dom mostly listened. She seemed to have swallowed her voice. What would Abuela think of what she'd done? She'd done exactly what she knew she shouldn't have.

The vet brought Dom out of her thoughts. "This little guy is hungry," she said. "It can't be more than two weeks old. And I bet you're right about the fox. I bet there are more kittens around too. Cats normally have more than one."

"That's what I was thinking," Steph said. "That's why I was coming back to get Dom—to help me look. And to try to find that howl."

Steph explained to Dr. Cabrera what they thought about the howl. "I counted it, this last time. Seven seconds between the first and the second. Seven seconds between the third and the fourth howls. It's a recording. I know if we find where the howl is coming from, we'll find Esther."

"You may be right. I'll tell you one thing," the vet said. "If someone went to the trouble of putting a recording to keep people away, they're taking care of Esther, right?"

Dr. Cabrera wasn't making sense. What did the recording have to do with taking care of Esther? The recording was meant to keep people away. If she hadn't fallen, they probably would have found Esther by now. Even though she was upset with herself and her bruise smarted, she wanted to keep looking.

She finally got her courage up. "Don't you think Steph's right? We should go back and look for that howl? We could find Esther tonight."

Dr. Cabrera answered Dom's question with one of her own. "You wanna fall in another hole?"

Dom shook her head.

Dr. Cabrera patted her on the back. "My dear

Sherlock," she said. "This time of day . . . too many shadows for a dangerous place like this. Tomorrow. Tomorrow we will find her. It's not worth risking another fall."

That was not what Dom wanted to hear. She felt even more miserable. She wanted to find Esther.

"I'll tell you what," the vet said. "Be at my house at six o'clock tomorrow morning. I'll take you into Lost Town. Safely. Ask your grandmother. If she's okay with it, I'll take you. The sun will be up high enough for us to see our way by then."

When they reached her house, the vet said, "Let me drive you home."

Dom was quick to answer. She wanted time to think. "No, no, really. I'm fine." She pointed to the sand still sifting through her clothes. "I'll make a mess of your car. And you need to take care of the baby."

Dr. Cabrera hesitated.

"It's okay," Steph said. "I know how to get us home quickly from here. We can just cut through the backyards, right? We'll be at Gran's house in five minutes."

Dr. Cabrera let Steph and Dom pat the kitten goodbye before she opened the door to her porch.

It should have been a five-minute walk, but to Dom it felt like forever. How could she tell Gran what she'd done? Worse, how could she tell Abuela?

7
What Happened
That Night

Gran was waiting at the door.

"I'm sorry," Dom said the minute she stepped onto the porch. "We really wanted to find Esther, and we thought we were close to finding her and maybe there was a hound, except probably there wasn't but maybe there was and we didn't want Esther to get hurt or spend another night out in Lost Town, and we went to Lost Town, but it was for a good reason. And I fell. It was all my fault. We shouldn't have gone."

"That's what I was afraid of," Gran said.

"Steph didn't want to go. It was me. It was all my fault."

"But you're all right?"

Dom nodded.

"That's what really matters." Gran gently brought them around to the mudroom and pulled down some towels from a shelf. "Here you go. Leave all that sand here. I'll have the best soup in the world ready for you after you take a nice hot shower."

🔍🔍🔍

Dom let the hot water run over her body. It washed off the sand. And the dirt. But not the guilt. She still felt awful. It was true Sherlock Holmes often took big, big chances. But he always knew what he was doing. Why had they gone to Lost Town? Why didn't she take the time to think things through?

🔍🔍🔍

"Here's some Brunswick stew." Gran put a steaming bowl of beans, veggies, and chicken in front of each of them. It smelled delicious! She gave each girl a huge chunk of yellow bread. "And Sally Lunn bread is the best thing to crumble into it."

Steph picked up her spoon and tackled the stew in the same way Dom would tackle her favorite: black beans and rice. Gran chattered on as she served herself.

"I want to hear all about it. Tell me what you found out about Esther."

The girls told their story.

"How lucky that you rescued the kitten! You'll have to go visit it in the morning. Maybe we could help Dr. Cabrera take care of it while we're here."

That gave Dom a little bit of hope. Gran still didn't seem mad at her.

During dessert, the girls told Gran about Dr. Cabrera's offer to take them to Lost Town to look for Esther early in the morning.

"Of course, of course," Gran agreed. "That's a

great idea. She and Birdie Ballou are old friends. She can show you exactly where to step. Or if it turns out she has a critter that needs help and she can't go, you should call Marabella. She'll be happy to help you. I'm sure of it."

Dom was sure Marabella would help them too. But she wasn't sure she'd help the way Gran thought. On the other hand, Gran was not mad. Not at all.

While waiting for Pancho to get back from the restaurant, Dom left a message for Rafi. She told him they'd taken lots of notes and lots of pictures. Then she called Abuela. She told her the whole story.

"I fell in a sinkhole, but I'm fine. Just one great big bruise. You ought to see it." She hoped that by laughing at it, Abuela wouldn't get mad at her.

"Ay, mi amor, qué miedo."

"It was *scary*. Steph was off looking at something else. She didn't hear me call for help. I was lucky the vet we talked to earlier was looking for Esther and she saw me. She pulled me out."

"How could—how could this Gran-woman let you go to a place like that? And how could Steph leave you?" Dom heard what Abuela was thinking—Steph's grandma was careless—before knowing all the facts.

"It was my fault, Abuela. She told us not to go. Not by ourselves. I was the one who wanted to go. Steph didn't. We weren't planning on going very far. But I guess we got carried away. And besides, Steph was rescuing a kitten. That was important," Dom explained.

"Of course it's important to rescue a goat. And a kitten. But you need to be careful."

"I'm okay, really. Don't worry."

"I always worry, preciosa. I always worry," Abuela said softly.

All of a sudden the feelings of the day crushed her. Dom wanted to cry. Her eyes filled. Her throat was tight and scratchy. She sniffled. "I'm sorry, Abuela. I'm really sorry."

"Well," Abuela said after a few seconds of silence. When she spoke, her tone was much lighter. "The good thing is that you're fine. Is Steph's grandmother mad at you?"

"She doesn't seem to be."

"Well, then. You're lucky that she's not. And you're lucky you're all right. And I hope tomorrow you'll find that goat!"

And that. Was that. And the honor of the Cuban children in the universe was still untouched.

"Thank you, Abuela."

"Always, mi amor."

"I have to go now, okay? It's time to call Pancho. We have to figure out how to solve this problem."

"Adios, mi amor. Besitos." Abuela blew a kiss on FaceTime.

"Besitos, Abuela." Dom returned the kiss with a big, happy smack.

What They Figured Out

"So what do we know?" Dom said after she and Steph had told Pancho everything that had happened.

Steph brought out the pages she'd torn from the notebook. She started ticking off their findings. "We are pretty sure a fox killed a mama cat, and there are probably other kittens hiding in Lost Town. I'll put that in the WHAT WE KNOW page."

"I think we can safely say now that Marabella and the little boy stole Esther," Pancho said. "You guys saw them together. And she's been acting funny."

"Yes," Dom said. "We can say that."

"I don't think they stole her," Steph said. "What if—what if they found the other kittens! You know—if there were three or four. We found one, and they found the others. Then they *borrowed* Esther for her milk? Remember what Dr. Cabrera said? She had frozen goat milk in the freezer just for animals, like the kittens."

Dom's mouth dropped. Steph was the one making the Sherlock Holmes deductions.

"But Marabella could just steal some milk without taking Esther," Pancho said. "It would be much easier to do that. And it would be just as easy to ask Mrs. Ballou. I'm not buying that."

"What if—what if Marabella isn't mean? What if she's trying to do something nice?" Steph twirled her red hair with her pencil. "Like Doc Cabrera said her grandfather did? You know, help the criminal."

Dom didn't like the idea that Marabella was nice, but she went along with it. "Okay. If Marabella's nice, let's see how it could have happened. A little boy finds the kittens. He wants to keep them, for some reason." Dom tapped the page where Steph was writing. "He might want a pet."

"And, for some reason, he can't tell his parents about the kittens," Steph added.

"And he figures out that the kittens need milk because their mama is gone." That was Pancho.

"So he borrows Esther. That all fits in with the milk pail, reaching for the leash with a stick, and the small flip-flop print on the marsh," Sherlock Dom had to add. "So then he'd be all set!"

"But what if—what if he doesn't know how to milk Esther! He needs a friend. A friend who knows how to milk a goat!" Steph asked.

"MARABELLA!" they all yelled.

"But why doesn't Marabella bring Esther back and turn the boy in?"

"Maybe it's just because she's nice," Steph said again. "If she brings the goat back and doesn't tattle, *she'll* get in trouble. If she tattles, *he'll* get in trouble."

Everybody was saying that Marabella was nice! Dom didn't want to believe that. "Wait, wait. Marabella's not nice!"

"She could be," Pancho said from the phone.

"Gran said she was nice," Steph said. "About three weeks ago, Mrs. Ballou was sick and Marabella was the one who called her son and stayed with her until he came. Gran told me."

"And that's the only way it works, Sherlock," Pancho said. "If she's nice."

"Hrmph!" If what they all said was true, the vet was right. Marabella was gruff on the outside and soft on the inside. But still. "Why is she doing all this Sherlock Holmes stuff?"

"Maybe Gran is right. We're doing Sherlock Holmes stuff. And she's doing Sherlock Holmes stuff back—playing with us. At least she didn't sic a dog smeared with Day-Glo paint on us!" Steph said.

"Maybe she's good friends with the boy," Pancho said. "And we're right. She doesn't want him to get in trouble, so she's using Sherlock Holmes to keep us away."

Dom was having a really hard time giving up the idea of Marabella as a villain. "At least she's an accessory to the crime," she said.

"That means she helped out," Pancho explained without anyone asking. "But if they took Esther to save the kittens and they plan to return her, there's no crime."

Dom huffed. And huffed. Her shoulders slumped. Pancho was right. There was no crime. It would have been much more like Sherlock Holmes if there were a real crime. But it was starting to look like Pancho and Steph were right. Marabella was probably nice.

Still.

She could have a real Sherlock Holmes adventure without solving a crime, right? She took a deep breath. An idea was forming in her head. She and Pancho had saved bunnies during their knightly adventure. It wasn't spectacular, but it was good enough. Finding a goat and saving kittens was good enough too. And figuring out what happened was solving the problem. Maybe it wasn't a crime, but they were certainly solving a mystery. Sherlock Holmes solved mysteries too.

"You know?" she said. "We've forgotten something very important! Who is the little boy? We don't know that. It would have to be someone who knows Esther well."

"The only little boy I know around here lives next to Mrs. Ballou. . . . His name is Mikey. . . . Whoa! Why didn't I think of that?"

"Of course it's Mikey," Pancho said. "He knows Esther because he lives right next door. He knows Marabella because she milks Esther. He's probably watched Marabella milk Esther before. It looked easy, so he figured he could do it. And then he found out he couldn't."

"Wait a minute!" Dom said. "I've got it."

Steph stopped writing.

"What have you got?" Pancho said from the phone.

"You're right. Mikey found the kittens, and he borrowed Esther to save them. It also works that he asked for Marabella's help because he couldn't milk the goat himself. What I've got . . . what I've got . . . ."

"What have you got?" both Steph and Pancho yelled.

"I've got why Marabella didn't bring the goat back. Reason number one: Marabella thinks we're snooty, and at first she wanted to laugh at us. She didn't think we would even get close to figuring out where Esther was. Reason number two: she wants to show us she's as smart as we are, so she did all the Baskerville stuff. Reason number three, and the most important reason of all—drumroll, please . . . ."

"TA-DAH!!!"

"We're all over the place," Dom said. "There's no way Marabella and Mikey could bring the goat back because we're everywhere. And she thinks we're nasty and snooty and we wouldn't understand. She thinks we'll turn them in and they'll get in trouble."

"We'll have to show her!" Steph said.

"If she helped Mikey the way we think she did, she's proved to us that she's actually nice. Now we'll have to prove to her that *we're* actually nice." Dom had totally turned her thinking around. "We'll help them bring Esther back without getting them in trouble."

"In the morning."

"Bright and early."

"There's no way I can have the phone that early," Pancho said. "My mom listens to books while she walks."

"We've got this!" Dom said. And she put her arm around Steph.

9
What They Did the Next Day

Dom couldn't sleep. She woke up at one. She got up to pee at two. She went downstairs for a glass of water at three. Every time she got up, she looked through the window in Steph's room. It was as if something was calling her to that window. It had a direct line of sight through all the backyards on the Marsh Coast.

By four o'clock, she didn't even try to go back to sleep. She dressed quietly, pulled a chair to the window, and put her cheek to the glass. And she wasn't disappointed.

At exactly five o'clock, she saw it. A light along the backyards. In the moonlight, Dom could see a small person holding it.

"Steph," she whispered without taking her eyes off the figure.

Before Steph answered, a taller figure joined the other. Marabella and Mikey! It had to be.

Dom pushed her friend. "Steph, wake up. We have to go."

"What—what—time is it?"

"It's just five o'clock. But the game's afoot. The little boy and Marabella, they're on the way to Lost Town. And I was just thinking. What if they do something desperate because we're here and they don't know that we'd help them?"

"But Gran?" Steph had already changed into her shorts and was looking for a shirt.

In the seconds since she saw the two figures in the dark, Dom had worried about what Gran would say. But she had an idea. She'd cleared it with

Abuela in her mind, and Abuela had approved.

"We're going with Marabella. Gran said we could go with Marabella. She won't worry. We'll leave her a note."

They didn't have to.

Gran was already up, making ham biscuits for them. The two of them quickly told her they were going with Marabella. Gran pulled a humongous flashlight out of her pantry. She handed them a bottle of water each. "Be careful. Make sure Marabella waits for you."

The last part wasn't as easy as Gran would have wanted.

"If we shine the light on them, they'll get spooked," Dom said once they were outside.

Steph agreed, although she wanted to stick to what Gran had said. Really, the moon was still out, and it wasn't hard to see. It was the same path they'd taken on the way home the night before.

They followed the two figures along the backyards toward Lost Town. They were not afraid at all when they heard the howl of the pretend hound, even though it was spooky, spooky, spooky in the moonlight. They were so quiet, mice would have been louder.

They followed the grassy path to Lost Town for about ten minutes. But then the path narrowed. And got bumpy. They were close to where Dom fell.

Marabella and Mikey turned on a brighter flashlight. Dom and Steph had to turn on theirs.

Even though they pointed their flashlight straight down, the light still gave them away. The two figures

ahead of them stopped. And walked back to meet them.

Marabella flashed her bright light on the girls. "Didn't anyone teach you to mind your own business?"

"We want to help," Dom said.

"We know about the kittens and Esther. And we want to help you take care of them and return Esther," Steph added. "Without telling on anyone."

Although Steph was really good at making people

understand that she was being honest, Marabella wasn't believing her.

"What makes you think we need help?"

Dom stepped up. "We think you would have returned Esther earlier if we weren't here. We'll help you return her without anyone knowing about it. So no one will get in trouble. No one."

"And how will you do that?"

In that hour that she was up, looking out the window, Dom had given this a lot of thought. But should she tell them? Now Dom was thinking that Marabella might not listen to any of their ideas. She wouldn't blame the girl.

"We'll figure it out. All of us," Dom said. "Together. And we'll return her when no one's looking."

Marabella's eyes widened a bit, but she still looked suspicious.

"Wait," Dom said. "You need to know something. I wanted to think you stole Esther. I wanted to find Esther, and I wanted to solve the crime. But we've figured out that you're just trying to help Mikey and the kittens. Which is a good thing. Maybe if you give us a chance, you can figure out that we're all right too."

"Yeah. What about the kittens?" Mikey interrupted. "My kittens?"

"Hush," Marabella said. She sounded like a mother. "We'll figure that out too."

"Are the kittens okay?" Steph asked.

"I don't know." Marabella turned back toward Lost Town and shone her light on the path. The others followed. "They don't lap yet. Esther didn't have very much milk last night. They didn't look good when we left. She didn't either. That's another reason I didn't bring her back. I wanted to try to help her out."

"Maybe she hasn't had enough water," Steph said.

"No," Marabella said. "She didn't. The marsh water has too much salt. It would make her sick. We couldn't bring water last night because *someone* was here nosing around. It got too late."

"We have water," Steph said.

"We'll be glad to let her have it," Dom added.

"Mikey and I brought some too." Marabella lifted

a bag hanging from her shoulder. "And I brought baby bottles for the kittens. I just hope we're not too late."

"We're so sorry," Steph said. "We were only trying to help. We didn't know . . ."

"You shouldn't be so . . ."

"Snooty?" Dom finished.

Marabella laughed.

"We're almost there. Careful with this hole." She shone the big light on a plank. "Use that to walk over. Then make sure you step to the left. They're behind that wall there. The wall's safe."

The kittens were bundled in a pink blanket. They would have looked adorable. If their eyes were open. And bright. And their heads were moving. But at least their chests still moved up and down, breathing.

"We need to take them to Dr. Cabrera right now," Dom said. "She was about to bring us here. I'm sure she's up."

Mikey stopped them. "But she'll tell my mom! I need to show Mom that I can take care of them so she'll let me keep them. And the doc will make me get in trouble."

"Dr. Cabrera won't tell on you. We'll make sure she doesn't," Dom said. "But we have to take them now. They may not . . . They may not . . ."

"They have the best chance of being your pet if we take them to the vet," Steph said.

"Once they are better, then you can show them to your mom," Dom said. "We'll help you. We'll tell her what a good job you did."

That did it. Mikey picked up the kittens and handed them to Marabella. "You're the biggest, so you're the fastest. You take them."

"I'll make sure the doc's awake." Dom took off ahead of Marabella.

"Of course I'll take care of them," Dr. Cabrera said when Dom and Marabella told her the whole story. "Just like their brother. Did they get anything to eat?"

"Not much," Marabella said.

"Could we—could we use your back porch to plan?" Dom asked as Steph and Mikey joined them. "You know. So no one will know . . ."

"All yours," the vet said.

Dr. Cabrera showed them bagels, cream cheese, and several jars of jelly in the fridge. Then she pointed. "There's the toaster, the plates, the silverware, and the trash can's under the sink. Put your plates in the dishwasher when you're done. And take your time. This is the perfect place for clandestine operations." She zipped her mouth and winked.

"We'll lock the kitchen door when we leave," Dom said. It was what she would have said in Mundytown.

"Nobody locks doors around here," Marabella and the vet said together.

The vet picked up the kittens. "I'd better get these critters to my office now. I need to take care of them before my first appointment."

"Thank you. Thank you," the four of them said as she hurried to her car.

Steph called Gran and let her know they were with Marabella and it would be a little while before they came back. She told Gran they were having bagels at the vet's house.

"So what's the plan?" Marabella asked, still with a little challenge in her voice.

"What we need to figure out quickly," Dom said, "is whether we bring Esther back now, or wait until tonight." She asked a question that had been rolling around in her mind. "Mikey, you took Esther after Marabella milked her in the afternoon. We saw your prints behind Mrs. Ballou's house. What did you do? Did you take her to Lost Town in the dark?"

Mikey looked at Marabella as if asking for permission.

The older girl nodded.

At first Mikey spoke into his chest. "Marabella's brother and I found the kittens close to Lost Town about five o'clock. So we decided that we'd try to feed them and take care of them. And show that we could do it." The boy stopped talking.

But Dom was impatient. "So how did you get Esther?"

"Let him tell you," Marabella said. "It wasn't easy."

Now Mikey didn't want to talk.

"Okay," Marabella said. "I'll tell them. They hid the kittens inside Ichabod's garbage can fence. That's why he's afraid to tell you. Ichabod lives right there." She pointed to the house next to Dr. Cabrera's. "Ichabod was out of town, and Mikey's mom was taking the mail in for him. And garbage can fences are great places to hide. We use them for playing hide-and-seek all the time. But Ichabod's always yelling at us for cutting across his backyard."

Mikey took over his own story. "It was too late to go back to Lost Town. And we were afraid the fox would find them anyway. So we picked up Esther to get some milk. We couldn't get milk out of my fridge. My mom was right there. And the internet said goat's milk was good for them. We figured the kittens could nurse."

"So you just walked off with her?"

"Sure. We did it in the dark. We were gonna return her!"

Dom laughed. "Is that when you hid her behind the cattails?"

"Yeah. The light came on in Mrs. Ballou's house. We got back in the yard when she turned it off again. We brought Esther to Ichabod's garbage fence. The kittens wouldn't nurse, but I was able to get a little milk from her."

Marabella took over now. "That's when they heard Ichabod's garage door opening. He was two days early. They panicked. They brought the kittens and Esther to Mikey's house. To their garbage fence. They left them there until early in the morning, when they brought them to Lost Town."

"But I didn't want the fox to get them."

"So you recorded the howl to keep the fox away? It wasn't a Sherlock Holmes thing?"

Mikey nodded. "We recorded it onto my tablet that night. And we put it on a loop. One short howl and a longer howl and then repeat. Marabella's right. We got up really early and took them to Lost Town. We came this way. It was the quickest, shortest way. So we wouldn't get in trouble."

"Of course, they couldn't get any milk from Esther in the morning. That's when my brother told me about what they'd done. When you saw us in town. By then there was nothing we could do to return Esther."

"Because we were all over the place," Steph finished.

10

What Was under the Raincoat

"**W**ell, now we're working together, so let's figure it out," Dom said.

Mikey and Steph divided the tasks that were needed to help Esther—getting grain and hay and water back to Lost Town. Steph had shown that she knew a lot about Esther and goats. And Mikey knew about where Mrs. Ballou kept Esther's food. They'd have to make many trips, but Mikey knew a way they could do it without being seen.

"No!" Dom said, and then she remembered she shouldn't try to be bossy. Not without talking them into it first. "Sorry, wait. I'm thinking . . . I'm thinking . . . If we are going back and forth all day along the path and people see us, they'll think we're playing. We'll make sure they think we're playing. Then later, when we come back with Esther, they won't think anything about it."

"Why don't we just say that we found Esther?" Steph asked.

"I'm thinking the adults might start asking questions and then we'd have to lie and tell them we don't know, when we actually do know. And then they'll start thinking something's fishy and they'll really start checking it out." Dom shook her head. She had another reason, but she wasn't about to tell anyone. Sherlock Holmes always used drama. Turning in the goat wouldn't be dramatic at all. "We don't have to take that chance. Even if they don't find out anything, they'd think some of us did it and some of us are covering up."

"I agree," Marabella said. "They might not say

anything, but they'd think it. Everyone would think we did it." She scrunched her forehead for a second and then had another idea. "Why don't we just do it after dark?"

Dom had an answer ready. "Why didn't you do it after dark yesterday? Too dangerous, right?"

Marabella nodded slowly. "Maybe not for us . . . but maybe you're right. It's safer if we don't."

"Mikey already had to tell a story to get out of his house early this morning, right?"

Marabella laughed. "My brother spent the night with him the night before. He spent the night with us last night," she said. "We told my mom that I had to take him back home early this morning."

"See!" Dom said. "When you tell too many stories, moms start wondering."

"So how are you gonna bring Esther back in the middle of the day?"

"It doesn't have to be in the middle of the day," Steph said, although she didn't know what Dom was thinking.

"Exactly. Around five o'clock tonight, we bring Esther out of Lost Town while it's still kinda light. We can hide her in Dr. Cabrera's garbage fence." She had noticed that Gran had a garbage fence too, so she was sure Dr. Cabrera would have one. "Then we wait until it's really dark to bring her through the backyards."

"Can we go on the other side of the cattails?" Steph asked.

"I checked," Marabella said. "The tide is higher now. We'd get sucked in. Esther won't let you take her there anyway."

"Look," Dom said. "I have an idea of how to bring her out. I know where a raincoat is. Why don't we use a broom or something and dress it up with that raincoat. We drape it over Esther and we all walk with her."

"You don't have to put it on a broom!" Steph pointed to Marabella. "I bet we could make it so that Marabella could wear it. She holds Esther next to her, under the coat. And we all walk along with her. In a parade!"

Mikey jumped in. "So all day long, we'll parade around with Marabella in the coat, getting the stuff, and when it's time, we just put Esther under it!"

"That's even better!"

Marabella jumped up out of her chair. "What if it's too long for me?"

"Duct tape!" Dom answered. "We'll hem it with duct tape. It fixes everything. And we take it off as soon as we're done."

"We'll call it Operation Esther Rescue!" Steph said.

They gave each other high fives, cleaned up Dr. Cabrera's porch and kitchen, and agreed to meet again in two hours.

On her way back to Gran's, Dom thought about what they'd just learned. She had been wrong about so many things, but in the end they were able to get to the truth. They would rescue Esther and the kittens, and that was the important thing.

🔍🔍🔍

It worked exactly like they planned. They paraded back and forth during the day—Marabella in her slick, yellow raincoat, taking grain and water to Esther and

cleaning up the place in Lost Town, so no one would know Esther had been there. Esther was grateful. She ate the grain and hay with a huge grin on her face. Not even one light blinked in the neighborhood when they actually brought her back after dark.

Their story worked perfectly too. They told Gran and their parents that they were having pizza at Dr. Cabrera's. Because it was true. The vet actually invited them. For later.

While they ate, they called Pancho on Dom's phone and Rafi on Marabella's phone.

They told the whole story.

They hadn't finished eating the pizza from Pizza Palace when Mrs. Ballou called Dr. Cabrera. The vet put her on speakerphone and put her finger to her lips.

"She's back! She's back!" Mrs. Ballou said.

"See," the vet said. "I told you Esther knows her way around."

"I just can't imagine where she would have gone for so long!"

"You know . . ." The vet winked. "Goats never cease to surprise me. But I think it would be a good idea to put a spring on that gate so that it closes whenever you go in or out. And a secure latch, just to make sure."

"You're right. You're right."

"I'll send someone over tomorrow." The vet hung up on the happy goat owner.

They hung up with Rafi, but Pancho didn't want to go.

"Man, I wish I could go there. Lost Town and the marsh. That sounds like an amazing place."

"And they have two more days to get to know it," Marabella said. "I'll show them."

Dom hoped they could share Tapperville with Pancho someday. It had been a great adventure. She had not been a great Sherlock Holmes. But she had not been a great knight either. She had been good enough both times. And Steph! Steph was totally different in Tapperville than she had been in Mundytown. She had been much more than a sidekick during this adventure.

Dom was pretty sure she'd managed to uphold the honor of Cuban children everywhere. Marabella had even shown her a couple of things. And it had been just fine that she wasn't the boss of everything all the time.

She looked forward to a lot more adventures.

Author's Note

Dom thought of Sherlock Holmes as a real detective. She wasn't alone. Sherlock Holmes is a beloved character—the best detective ever—and the creation of Sir Arthur Conan Doyle, a Scottish physician who, like Dr. Watson, became a very successful writer. He wrote four novels and fifty-six short stories featuring the famous detective. Most of the short stories were published in the *Strand Magazine*. The novels appeared in chapters in the magazines and then again as books. They were all wildly popular. When, in 1893, Conan Doyle decided he was through with writing about Holmes, he had the detective die in a spectacular battle with his archenemy. Readers missed Holmes so much, however, that Conan Doyle decided to test the waters and write about Holmes again in stories that Watson "remembered." Finally, he had to bring the detective back to life.

Sherlock Dom is inspired by the story of *The Hound of the Baskervilles*. The story was the first that Conan Doyle wrote after he sent Holmes to an early grave. It was published between August 1901 and March 1902 in the *Strand Magazine*. The book came out that March. It is probably the most famous Sherlock Holmes adventure. After the success of *The Hound*, Conan Doyle brought his hero back to life.

Dom, like Sherlock Holmes, was antsy to solve problems. She also figured out things about people by just looking at them. They both wanted to get to the scene of the crime right away and became upset at people who erased clues by walking on them. Sherlock Holmes, like Dom did in the marsh, often fell or spilled something in order to take a look at a possible clue in detail without anyone realizing it.

For Sherlock Holmes, Watson was a sidekick. Someone to share in the adventure and help him when there might be danger. But Holmes often laughed at Dr. Watson's attempts at helping him, while Dom now recognized that Steph was smart in her own right and was an equal helper. Dom recognized that two brains were better than one and that working together made solving problems easier.

In most of the stories, Holmes helped an inspector from Scotland Yard, the British police. He helped Inspector Lestrade and others. In some instances, Holmes was respectful of the inspectors, while still knowing that he was superior. In other instances, Holmes quietly laughed at the inspectors. While Holmes solved the problem and never took credit, unlike Pancho, the inspectors didn't normally participate in solving the problem.

One thing Sherlock Holmes often did was decide that he knew better than the law. For instance, if someone got caught killing a really bad person, Sherlock Holmes would give the criminal the opportunity to get away. It was a little like what Dom did in helping Marabella and Mikey get away with "borrowing" Esther to save the kittens.

Conan Doyle wrote many books other than the Sherlock Holmes stories. They may have been better, or more important, but none were as popular as the stories of the world-famous detective.

Turn the page for a sneak peek
at Dominguita's first adventure!

Definitely
DOMINGUITA
★ Knight of the Cape ★

by Terry Catasús Jennings ★ illustrated by Fátima Anaya

A Dare

All Dominguita Melendez wanted to do today was read.

Her teacher, Mrs. Kannerpin, had encouraged her to "socialize" during recess. But Dominguita didn't want to socialize. She always had adventures to go on and new characters to meet. She ought to be able to read, right? Other kids got stars for reading *one* book, after all. And today, more than any other day, Dominguita just wanted to read.

It didn't look like she would be able to do what she wanted, though. Not with Ernie Bublassi heading her way.

"Krankypants wants you to join the game," he said.

Why couldn't Mrs. Kannerpin leave her alone? And why had she sent the biggest jerk in her grade to find her?

"She said someone needed to look for you, and I volunteered," Ernie said.

Great. He could read her mind.

"She wants you to come play dodgeball."

"Ugh." Dominguita slammed her book shut.

Ernie shrugged. "Everybody knows you read 'cause you don't have any friends."

"Huh? I do so have friends!" Dominguita's fists clenched.

"Who?"

She wanted to tell Ernie Bublassi the names of all her friends, but since Miranda moved to a place called Pascagoula in second grade, she'd been too busy reading to find any more friends.

"I don't need friends," she said, even though she still missed Miranda. "I'm studying to be a knight."

The minute she said it, she knew she was in trouble. *BIG trouble*. And it was all because Ernie Bublassi knew how to make her mad. And angry. And upset. And furious.

He grabbed her book. "A knight! *You* studying to be a knight? Girls can't be knights! I never heard of any girl-knights."

Dominguita would gladly have told him about Joan of Arc—she was a kind of knight, right? There must have been others. Dominguita was sure. But there was only one thing on her mind.

"Give it back! That's my grandmother's book!"

"Oh yeah? You studying to be an old-lady knight?" Ernie Bublassi threw the book in the playground dirt. "You'll never be a knight."

"I can *too* be a knight. I'll show you! And you are the meanest person in the universe!"

She picked the book up as if it were holy. And it was. It was one of the things her grandmother loved best, and right now Dominguita couldn't think of anything she loved more. She stomped toward the dodgeball game. It was the only way she would get rid of Ernie Bublassi.

But Ernie Bublassi wasn't through with her.

"Hey, guys!" he yelled as they reached the dodgeball game. "Dominguita's gonna be a knight. She's studying for it. A girl-knight. As if she wasn't weird enough already."